THE TIME TRAVELER

The group community
"American city"

Memory & memorials

Other books of poetry by Joyce Carol Oates

#1
61 poems in
4 sections

Anonymous Sins and Other Poems (1969)
Love and Its Derangements (1970)
Angel Fire (1973)
The Fabulous Beasts (1975)
Women Whose Lives Are Food,
    Men Whose Lives Are Money (1978)
Invisible Woman: New & Selected Poems 1970–1982 (1982)

Laurentian exclamations &
    interrogations

birds
feelings?

most beautiful
    "How Gentle" from
Love & Its Derangements

Joyce Carol Oates

THE TIME TRAVELER

A William Abrahams Book

E. P. DUTTON | NEW YORK

Published in the United States by E. P. Dutton,
a division of Penguin Books USA Inc.,
2 Park Avenue, New York, N.Y. 10016.

Published simultaneously in Canada
by Fitzhenry and Whiteside, Limited, Toronto.

Library of Congress Cataloging-in-Publication Data

Oates, Joyce Carol, 1938–
  The time traveler / Joyce Carol Oates.
    p.   cm.
  "A William Abrahams book."
  I. Title.
  PS3565.A8T49   1989   *89-7748*
  811'.54—dc20   *CIP*

ISBN: 0-525-24802-1 (cloth)
0-525-48505-8 (paper)

Designed by REM Studio

10 9 8 7 6 5 4 3 2 1

First Edition

For permissions and acknowledgments see page 129, which constitutes an ex-
tension of this page.

for Alicia and Jerry Ostriker

CONTENTS

I SAW
A WOMAN
WALKING...

I

LOVES OF THE PARROTS

Giant parrots of Yucatán perching
splendid in the sun! Bright green,
bright yellow, bright
arterial red!

Ruffling their beauty in tireless
search of lice! Picking
their toenails with imperial beaks!

Desire galvanizes the male
like an electric shock,
and there's the shriek
all females fear—
You! or *Here!* or *Now!* or
Why did you think you could escape me!

Such throes of love!
Mad eyes ringed in white!
Giant beaks hook
and crack,
bloody breast feathers go flying!
Bright green, bright yellow,
bright arterial red!

Love, not death, is the bitter thing.

YOUR BLOOD IN A LITTLE PUDDLE, ON THE GROUND

—for Leigh and Henry Bienen

"You aren't prepared for their quickness,
their tenacity. Their . . . numbers.
We were visiting a farm, and they were
throwing themselves against our feet,
dozens, hundreds—
I felt the vibrations against my boot,
the tapping heads, the mouths
drawn by the heat
of my blood."

"On the trek, I discovered one inside my shoe;
it had become a sort of conduit,
bloated with blood. It couldn't absorb
any more blood but it kept sucking, in one end and
out the other, and my shoe was filled, I mean filled
with my blood. . . . I still dream about it
sometimes."

"Some are thin as pencil points,
others the size of slugs.
They blow themselves up into long narrow balloons
with your blood."

4

"In the rainy season they're all over.
In the grass, in the mud; I've even seen them
crawling over rock.
They're rubbery and smart.
If you try to pick them off, they stick
to your fingers.
If you try to stomp them, they roll
themselves up into tiny balls
and hide in the rubber treads
of your boots, or in the lace holes
of your shoes. They like American jogging
shoes best."

"The Nepalese farm workers in the fields,
in the wet grass, barefoot, bare-legged
to the thigh—'Oh, they're immune,'
we were told. And: 'Their advantage is
they can see them
and pull them right off.'
And: 'They're not like us;
they don't mind losing
a little blood.' "

"If you pour salt on them the salt won't kill
them, but if you add water to the salt
they dissolve. It's very . . . strange.
And your blood's there, suddenly,
on the ground. Returned to you
in a little puddle. On the ground."

SELF-PORTRAIT AS A STILL LIFE

The nude sprawling lazy inside the antique gilt frame.
The fleshy nude asleep inside the antique gilt frame.
Inside the gilt frame the lazy boneless body.
The nude in humid sunshine inside the gilt frame.
The nude voluptuous stroking a blue guitar,
ripe melons for breasts. Inside the heavy gilt frame.

The nude with shameless limbs asprawl inside the gilt frame.
The nude with grapes for eyes inside the gilt frame.
Inside the gilt frame the nude yawning into a mirror.
The nude blown up plump and merry as a child's balloon.
Dimples, patchy hair, persimmon mouth, inside the gilt frame.
The nude hanging head downward from a meat hook,
inside the gilt frame.

That big strapping husky good-hearted girl!—inside the gilt
     frame.
The eyes staring without pupils, listening hard,
inside the heavy gilt frame. The nude surprised in sleep!
Inside the gilt frame, the nude posed prettily with a
     paper mandolin.
O do not hurt me, please hurt me, have you a name,
please don't leave me here alone—inside the gilt frame.

The nude perspiring rich globules of oil inside the gilt frame.
Dimpled, the nude starving to death inside the gilt frame.
O love me, please worship me, please do not injure me,
inside the gilt frame. Has this place a name?
Inside the gilt frame the nude brazen showing wisps
         of hair
beneath her stretched arms. Yawning. Tears spilling down
her cheeks. Inside the gilt frame, the air turned to steam.

The nude that is a deft pencil sketch inside the gilt frame.
The nude that is a basket of ripe plums inside the
         gilt frame.
O do not despise me, please forgive me, I am guilty,
I have always been ashamed. Inside the gilt frame.
The nude as the Virgin Mary inside the ancient gilt frame.

The nude reclining voluptuous amid the waxy apples,
inside the gilt frame. I swear I have never been hungry,
I swear I am innocent of appetite, O please do not
         strangle me.
Inside the gilt frame the nude who is pink rubber and
         rose nipples.

The nude stroking a Persian kitten inside the gilt frame.
The nude leering with pupil-less eyes inside the gilt frame.
The nude starving to death inside the gilt frame.
The nude peeling a sensuous fat orange inside the gilt frame.

I SAW A WOMAN WALKING INTO A PLATE GLASS WINDOW

I saw a woman walking into a plate glass window
as if walking into the sky.

I saw her death striding forward to meet her,
shadowed in flawless glass.

Dogwood blossoms drew her, a lilac-drugged air,
it was beauty's old façade,
blinding,
blind: the transparency
that, touched, turns opaque.

The frieze into which she stepped buckled in anger
and dissolved in puzzle parts about her head.

   •   •   •

I saw a woman walking into sunshine confident and composed
and tranquil to the last.

I saw a woman walking into *something* that had seemed *nothing*.
As we commonly tell ourselves.

The trick to beauty is its being unassimilable,
a galaxy of glittering reflections,
each puzzle part in place.
Not this raining of glass and blood
about the amazed head.

The *unfathomable depths* into which she stepped became
the merest surface,
Pain and noise.

•   •   •

I saw a woman walking into her broken body
as if she were a bride.

I saw her soul struck to the ground because mere space
could not bear it aloft.

I saw how the window at last framed only *what was there,*
beyond the frame,
that could not fall.

My throat filled swiftly with blood:
you would not have believed how swiftly.

WHISPERING GLADES

They can't remember what brought them here.
In the slid-open door of the mobile home
sitting at 10 A.M. of a long morning,
her right leg braced with metal to the knee
and her face like a fine-wrinkled
glove furrowed in what you'd say was thought,
and dignity, furrowed with age, wisdom
engrained like the simplest grime
which she still, when she can,
detests. There's the flies, sometimes
I think the flies are the worst, she says,
I don't mean houseflies like back home I mean *flies*
the size of your actual thumb, and
they bite. Of course there's roaches
you sent me that clipping about,
from your newspaper, yes and they fly too,
terrible terrible things hitting
the screen. That rash on your grandfather's ankles
that's all red from him picking and scratching
at it, like he does, we think it's fleas
or something from that neighbor's damn dog—
'course it *is* a cute little thing, lonely
all day long—the girl at the clinic gave him
peroxide to put on it but what good's
that going to do, I told him for God's
sake, if he keeps on scratching.
But you know him, that old man,

you know *him* . . . can't tell him anything.
Those marigolds there, all that's left of them,
it's slugs that go after the poor things
but I love the smell, you know that smell?
I love it. Like the tomato plants,
the leaves, that kind of smell,
but they didn't last in those damn pots
like we were told, the tomato worms got them
but don't get me started on *them;*
makes me sick just to think
about it. The things that happen
when you're my age, and all you
remember that can come back, flooding
your head, you know, like, what's-it,
a backed-up sink or something. Something
worse! Don't get me started! She's laughing,
This here is you kids' vacation and all,
but Christ, if you knew what's coming!
If you knew . . . but you're too young.
Everything's too damn easy for you kids, now.

PLAYLET FOR VOICES

May I serve you? This is delicious. Please sit anywhere. Please take off your coats. You are very generous. You are very sweet. Is it still snowing out? We're so grateful. Has everyone been introduced? Shall I take your coats? Just slip your gloves in here. Thank you very much. Please pass it on. Please come back soon. This *is* delicious. Is the walk icy? Can you find your way? Let's close the door quickly!

Will you have another serving? Why won't you have another serving? Thank you very much. It doesn't matter, please sit anywhere. We are in the habit of sitting anywhere. It is a custom to sit anywhere. Thank you very much, this is delicious, may I have the recipe? Is it cold outside? Can you find your way?

Siblings and parents (it is said) devour every second child in order to gain "mystical strength." Among the Pitjantjara tribe of Australia. Yes, thank you. You are so generous. We're so grateful to be invited. Yes, that is her likeness on the wall. *Thank* you. You are exceptionally kind. Will you have another serving—and pass it on? There is a theory that they devour their infants partly for reasons of "nourishment" as well but it's farfetched, isn't it, since an infant only a few days old is a minimal feast indeed. Except if it is named. If they have given it a name. No, I don't suppose baptism—they wouldn't be that advanced. Would they be that advanced? But if it has a name then it can't be eaten. If it has a name then it is safe from its parents and siblings and can't be eaten. Why do you suppose that is? What curious customs! Some people will believe anything they are told!

Actually they are artificial flowers. Actually they are primroses and not "roses." Would you like to sit here? Has everyone been introduced? Has everyone had a second helping? It must be freezing outside. It's warmer by the fire. Let's adjourn to the other room. Coffee, brandy. Where are our coats? Whose gloves are these? She died suddenly. One of the physicians commented on morbid obesity. It was a lingering death as many are but, at the end, sudden: That is often the case. How can we be responsible for aboriginal behavior in Australia?

May I serve you? Is this smoke annoying you? May I take your coat? Why must you leave so early? Yes, but we must leave. But you have just arrived. Thank you *very* much, we are all extremely grateful.

Have you all been introduced? It was a merciful death as deaths go these days. Please take another serving, you haven't eaten anything. There is more than enough for everyone. Three days' preparation have gone into this meal. She was secretly disappointed. That is often the case. This is certainly a privilege—where will you sit? *This* is delicious. Why are you shivering? Come sit by the fire. Have you all been introduced? It is ten-thirty. It is so frequently ten-thirty. Death was said to have been caused by heart failure. It is always ten-thirty in this room. Why must you leave so early? Thank you *very* much. Please come back soon.

This is exquisite: May I have the recipe? You are very sweet to have invited us. She has been dead now—oh, I'd say more than a year: fifteen months at least. Is it eighteen months? Yes, it is a good likeness. Yes, some traits are misleading. The roses *are* beautiful but they are not ours. Actually they are primroses. Please have another serving and pass it on. Is the bowl too hot? Must you leave so early? Has everyone been introduced? But you have just arrived. But we are very grateful. Yes, these *are* my gloves.

AN ORDINARY MORNING IN LAS VEGAS

—for David Lehman

My right hand's a claw from the slots.
You get so you don't even love it.
"One Thousand Coins Jackpot" was playing when he died.
She wept, her hair was on fire.

You get so you don't even love it—
there's a place of stasis beyond desire.
She wept, her hair was on fire.
Fruits and germs gaily spinning in the pit.

There's a place of stasis beyond desire
but you must wash your hands every hour.
God spins his fruit here. *And his germs.*
The blackjack lady has all the power.

You must wash your hands every hour.
"No brotherhood," he sighed, "like craps."
The blackjack lady has all the power.
but complains—diminution of desire!

"No brotherhood," he sighed, "like craps."
The croupier's an Eisenhower heir
but complains of diminution of desire.
Germs breed in mucus, coin, and hair.

The croupier's an Eisenhower heir.
Eight decks of cards in *his* power!
Germs breed in mucus, coin, and hair so
you must wash your hands every hour.

"One Thousand Silver Coins" played at his cremation.
The roulette wheel?—gummed up with lox.
We love each other beyond death, she said—but
my right hand's a claw from the slots.

You must wash your hands every hour.
You must wash your hands every hour.
You must wash your hands every hour.
You *must* wash your hands every hour.

WELCOME TO DALLAS!

Welcome to Dallas!—this place is wild!
Nothing's more than five years old!
24 HAPPY HOURS 'ROUND THE CLOCK!
He died, his lungs was Dutch Boy Glitter-Gold!

Nothing's more than five years old—
our city bird's the CONSTRUCTION CRANE!
He died, his lungs was Dutch Boy Glitter-Gold!
Nothing's been built that can't be sold!

Our city bird's the CONSTRUCTION CRANE!
InterFirst Plaza & ThanksGiving Square!
Nothing's been built that can't be sold!
Dallas/Ft. Worth Airport is bigger than Zaire!

InterFirst Plaza & ThanksGiving Square!
World Trade Center & John Neely Bryan Restored Log Cabin!
Dallas/Ft. Worth Airport is bigger than Zaire!
"When we got there, we forgot where we were going!"

World Trade Center & John Neely Bryan Restored Log Cabin!
OOOOOOOhhhhhh man—it's how you *fly!*
"When we got there, we forgot where we were going!"
The custom-built helicopter's here a *habit!*

OOOOOOOhhhhhh man—it's how you *fly!*
One good huff of Black Flag you want to *die!*
The custom-built helicopter's here a *habit!*
"When we got there, we forgot where we were going!"

One good huff of Black Flag you want to *die!*
When the going gets tough the tough go shopping!
Drinks in Deep Ellum, you forget where you've *been!*
See my new Nieman-Marcus boots made for STOMPING!

When the going gets tough the tough go SHOPPING!
The MOON so dam' big you step on his dam' FACE!
See my new Nieman-Marcus boots made for STOMPING!
The Ferrari headlights flashed and there shone—
         NO DUMPING!

The MOON so dam' big you step on his dam' FACE!
We'll rendezvous in bankruptcy court—just in case!
The Ferrari headlights flashed and there shone—
         NO DUMPING!
Is there a life, she pondered, after shopping?

We'll rendezvous in bankruptcy court—just in case!
Pittsburgh Black & Dutch Boy Glitter-Red!
Is there a life, she pondered, after shopping?
"Hector looked so peaceful, how'd we know he was dead?"

We didn't smell no thing, man, the Rodriguez family said!
All them smells, man, already in the air!
"Hector looked so peaceful, how'd we know he was dead?"
Airplane glue & turpentine & Day-Glo Glitter-Red!

Welcome to Dallas!—this place is wild!
(She talked so cool, man, how'd we know she was a
    child!)

LOVE LETTER, WITH STATIC INTERFERENCE FROM EINSTEIN'S BRAIN

Some say the world is Numbers, some say the world is a Mouth, but when you are in love such observations possess very little weight. And while it is perhaps true that most women are in (undiagnosed) terror of bleeding to death, it is historically true that they have put their terror to good use in cultivating the art of the *warm and engaging smile.*

For instance, let me share with my love the sudden realization that: this rural landscape possesses the fey asymmetrical charm of a vision seen through the bottom of a Coca-Cola bottle!—for so it *does* suddenly seem.

For instance, though some say the world is Numbers, and some say the world is a Mouth, how can science explain the fact that if, at this moment, I approach the mirror on my wall, and raise my right hand, *it is really my left hand I am raising in the mirror?* (In fact I am acting out this experiment right now.) (I have acted out this experiment while composing my letter.)

Many wild stories circulate in this neighborhood about Einstein's brain and its influence, years after his death. However, my love, I hope not to worry you because *I am well and have never felt better in my life.* As for the theory that women are in (undiagnosed) terror of bleeding to death, and draining away like cracked vases, it is wisest to contemplate the food heaped on your plate and give thanks to the Almighty that it is on *your* plate and not someone else's on the far side of the globe. You have a warm and engaging smile. Thank you, I have a dimpled smile. Thank *you*, I have a sweet smile. I have a charming smile, thank you. *Thank you*, I have a luminous smile. Thank you, I am blessed with a fetching smile. I, a shy smile. I, a guileless. You are very observant, thank you, I have a dazzling smile. Thank *you*, I have a madcap smile arranged to show eleven teeth. Though some say the world is Numbers, and some say the world is a Mouth.

My love, do not be jealous of the brain's interference because I am untouched by it, though sometimes the air reeks of formaldehyde when the wind blows from a certain direction. And do not be jealous when I confess that, Tuesday afternoon, I encountered a former lover at a banquet. The poor creature had aged greatly and did not recognize me at first. All his hair had fallen out, the secret wink in his left eye had become a twitch, his sullen overweight nineteen-year-old daughter sat beside him cutting his meat into small pieces, shaking dollops of sour cream on his baked potato, lighting his cigarettes, etc. "If I suffer from a degenerative disease," the poor creature said, with an attempt at his old jocose humor, "does that make me a degenerate?"

Though some say the world is Numbers, no one wishes to speculate as to their sum if they are added up. It is more tempting to gossip about the bootlegged brain in our midst, and to match our footsteps with the famous "ghost footsteps" on the graveled path leading to Einstein's former residence. Oh, it *is* tempting!—but I have not succumbed.

It is dangerous to take yourself too seriously because Einstein has proven that you cannot conceive of an idea that vast, for if the candle flame is snuffed out, *had it ever existed?—and how could its existence be demonstrated?* Yet, it is dangerous to take yourself too lightly because then strangers will brush rudely past you, not minding if they knock you aside, and even your loved ones will one day cease to recognize you. My love, why have I not heard from you in fourteen years?

Some say the world is a Mouth but our local genius was not one of them. Numerous people in the village tell warm and humorous anecdotes concerning him to this day, such as: the gnarled old cobbler on Bedlam Lane for whom Einstein did his income tax several years in succession; the Negro groundskeeper (now greatly aged) who tended the grass along Philosopher's Walk for whom Einstein always had a kind word; the pack of apple-cheeked schoolboys (now grown into mature adults) whom Einstein helped with their arithmetic homework . . . *sometimes making little errors!* Everyone recalls his snowy-white hair, his boyish smile, his brain still snugly encased in its skull, the creak of his bicycle, which often needed oiling. My love, I absorb myself in harmless local legends while awaiting your arrival.

You laughed in delight and kissed me. You laughed gaily and recklessly and kissed me hard. I kissed your pursed lips. You kissed mine and took my breath away. You, you laughed defiantly and seized me in an embrace and kissed me *as a man kisses a woman.* I kissed you in return *as a woman kisses a man* because my thoughts were wholly on you and not elsewhere. You boldly kissed my lips. You laughed puckishly and kissed my lips *hard.* As a man kisses a woman, so you kissed me, while focusing your thoughts upon me. As a woman kisses a man, so I kissed you, while focusing my thoughts upon you, despite the faint odor of formaldehyde.

I will love you forever, you said. Thank you, I will love *you* forever. I will die for you! Thank you, I will die for *you.* You are beautiful. Thank you, you are handsome. You are ravishingly beautiful. *You,* you are ravishingly handsome. I have never met anyone like you before. I have never met anyone like *you* before. Why is this landscape blurred, as if glimpsed through the bottom of a Coca-Cola bottle? It is gray and overcast,

24

resembling a landscape glimpsed through the bottom of a Seven-Up bottle. I will love you forever. Thank you, I will love *you* forever until one of us dies.

Some say the world is Numbers, some say the world is a Mouth, but it is a world of *morality, law,* and *simple human interaction* as well, in which case it was wicked for an unauthorized surgeon to secretly remove Einstein's brain from his skull and hide it away beneath a cellar stairs, when the great physicist-genius had stated his wish beforehand that he did not want an autopsy. His wish was for cremation, which all the world knows.

He flexed his manly fingers and we both stared at them, against our conscious intention. These were the fingers (strong, stubby, manly, with clean square forthright nails) that had held Einstein's brain; but they very much resembled any fingers. Why is so much in life taken for granted, I cried suddenly, so that other strollers in the garden turned to stare; when it so transparently partakes of the miraculous?

It is futile and silly to fritter away your life in terror that you will soon bleed to death, and far more practical to heap everyone's plate high with steaming food and insist upon second helpings. I have always counted myself proudly among the latter. For if the world is Numbers someone else will add them up, and if the world is a Mouth it must be fed.

My love, it has been so long. It seems like yesterday. Surely I have seen your face before?—it is a haunting and unforgettable face. I await a message or a signal from you, in plain English or (if you prefer) in code. I have forgotten nothing. Yes, but you have dropped your fragrant nosegay on the path. I stroll about at dusk, at the "violet" hour, alert to emanations in the breeze. My love, you *will* live forever. *And so will I.*

(He weighed it in his two hands, he said smiling. Was it uncommonly heavy?—it was not. Was it uncommonly large?—it was not. Did it possess any uncommon features?—it did not. "It was a brain like any other," he said. "Though it reeked now of formaldehyde. And had turned slightly pale from being so long in its jar beneath the cellar stairs. It had," he said thoughtfully, "been dead a long time.")

LUXURY OF BEING DESPISED

In revenge and in love, women are
more barbaric than men.
                    —Nietzsche

The sneering shout in the street, the anatomical female
stretched wide across the billboard: St. Paul's contempt.

Montaigne instructs us that poetry belongs to women—
a wanton and subtle art, ornate and verbose,
all pleasure
and all show: like themselves.
And Freud, that women have little sense of justice.
And De Kooning, in these angry swaths of paint:
crude and magnificent, these monster women!

The fiery sightless eye which is your own.
The booming breasts, the maniac wink.
All is heat, fecundity, secret seeping blood.
Flesh is here: *nor are we out of it.*

           What bliss, to be so despised:
the closed thighs all muscle,
the Church Fathers' contempt,
the Protestant chill, what freedom
to have no souls!—
what animal delight.

The angry swaths of flesh which are your own.
The blank stare,
the cartoon heart.
Virginity a mallet.
Mad grin worn like a bonnet.

PEACHES, PINEAPPLES, HAZELNUTS . . .

Women are fruits. There are peaches,
pineapples, and hazelnuts. No need
to continue: it is clear.
—Paul Valery, *Mélange*

No need to continue, it is clear
how ecstatic we are you're dead,
though we must not say so, but compose
our faces otherwise. Though Death
is that marbled world of Absence
we cannot enter. We lead you to it
but we cannot enter. Peaches, pineapples,
hazelnuts, oranges, grapefruits, red
apples and golden apples and tart greeny
apples, apricots, plump black cherries,
sour red cherries, plums and prunes and
raisins, avocados, nectarines, kumquats,
skin and all, sweet pulpy bananas, pears
and papaya, persimmons and pomegranates,
rhubarb, blueberries and blackberries and
huckleberries and raspberries, straw-
berries, lemons, limes, mangoes, kiwi,
cantaloupe, and watermelon so watery, crude,
no need to continue but I love best

this sweet heavy Persian melon with its
fleshy meat like the softest skin
of the inner thigh, so many seeds and all
so sweet, subtle as the most judicious
of poisons.

WHITE PIANO

—for Elliott Gilbert

Unrequited love is wisest, it fattens
the heart. So seat yourself
at the white piano.

Begin by depressing a single note—
the G above middle C, for instance.

White of gardenias floating in dream
pools, hot ice, something whitely
scalding your veins to transparence.
Ah, exquisite!—beyond your reckoning.

Now a chord. Now the scale of C major,
which you learned when you were ten.
And now the scale of C minor, which is trickier.
Have you grown trickier?
Sad to contemplate the piano teachers
you outlived, but still
your fingers are happiest here
at the white piano, where
even mistakes sound good.

      White octaves, white
triads, white diminished sevenths, white arpeggios—
why do such useless feats
command the most devotion? For here

your fingers *are* quicker than your soul, witty, gay,
somber (when required)—
exuberant too and shameless, as when you play
Mozart's "Alla Turca" and your gray Persian rises
quietly and leaves the room.

Now you contemplate some Chopin!—and surely this is
the best part: contemplation.
That slow second Prelude, C major to break
the heart, you'd once learned to perfection then
heard played in a Bergman film where
it sounded conspicuously different. But
as I've said, unrequited love
is wisest. Seated at the white piano,
where all you've wished for will be granted you,
could you give it a name.

DON'T BARE YOUR SOUL!

—for Coleen Grissom

Don't bare your soul to anyone, however gentle,
    solicitous, seductive, or wise!
Don't do it! Don't
    make that mistake!
Don't bare your soul and leave it to be scarified
    like a Formica-topped table!
Greasy and wrinkled like an old dollar bill!
Blown like dirty confetti along the pavement!

Remember the long letter you wrote in anguish and self-
    laceration, out of conscience unsparing as a steel
    comb, up half the night, head packed in pain,
    and no answer ever came! None!
And the book inscribed *In deepest love* you saw tossed
    amid family trash in the rear of a Honda hatchback,
    with that melancholy look of a book never once
    opened! And why should it have been opened,
    your soul so yearning and bared?

And the long dreamy talk you once had, hand folded
    into hand, feet clasping feet for warmth, pulse-
    beats in equilibrium as, at dusk, as dusk deepens,
    the interior darkness expands to meet the exterior,
    and there is a breathless moment when both are equal:
    that came to nothing in the end—as you should
    have known!

So don't bare your soul in intimacy, still less
    in company!
Don't do it! Don't
    make that mistake!
Don't bless while being cursed!
Remember that Hell is memory with no power of alteration,
    remorse that is one-sided merely, shame a mirror
    showing only your face.
Don't bare your soul to anyone, no matter who invites it!
No matter who whispers, I will love you forever—tell me
    all your secrets!
Don't do it!
And if you do it, don't talk about it!
Not even to yourself!
And don't write about it!
    Especially not that!

"I DON'T WANT TO ALARM YOU"

II

MARSYAS FLAYED BY APOLLO

In this late great oil by Titian, the satyr
Marsyas is being flayed alive, hanging upside
down from a tree. What technique is required
we have to guess, skinning a fellow creature alive;
what surgical precision, patience, craftsmanly
pride—the usual secrets
of someone's trade.

Does it require practice, or can it
be done properly the first time?

WINSLOW HOMER'S *THE GULF STREAM*, 1902

If there is a God of the Gulf it is a God
        of water, not waves but water,
all the globe turned water-pocked, ris-
        ing and falling tireless, for-
ever. Here is your story.

The Bahamas, the aftermath of a storm.
        On the deck of a small heaving fish-
ing sloop lies a Negro, superbly muscled,
        doomed, bucking the waves
of the Gulf Stream which are china-

blue, notched like the fins, tails,
        and teeth of white sharks
following in his wake. The sloop's mast
        has broken off. The waves
are tinged with blood.

The sharks appear to be cavorting
        like porpoises, but we know
that if there is a God of the Gulf
        it is a God of crazed beauty
and appetite, a gut with teeth,

a painted form you might say like
        any other. Art's great terrible

truth composed in brush strokes out of
    so many small lies.
To the right of the canvas, in the back-

ground, there is a funnel of water rising
    dreamily out of the sea to no purpose.
And though on the horizon a ship has appeared—
    ghostly, four-masted, story-
book—it cannot save the doomed man,

it is irrelevant to his story. With what
    composure he stares off the canvas,
indifferent to his fate! As if, long
    ago, he'd memorized all the forms
of the Gulf, now it is time to forget.

EDWARD HOPPER'S *NIGHTHAWKS,* 1942

The three men are fully clothed, long sleeves,
even hats, though it's indoors, and brightly lit,
and there's a woman. The woman is wearing
a short-sleeved red dress cut to expose her arms,
a curve of her creamy chest; she's contemplating
a cigarette in her right hand, thinking that
her companion has finally left his wife but
can she trust him? Her heavy-lidded eyes,
pouty lipsticked mouth, she has the redhead's
true pallor like skim milk, damned good-looking
and she guesses she knows it but what exactly
has it gotten her so far, and where?—he'll start
to feel guilty in a few days, she knows
the signs, an actual smell, sweaty, rancid, like
dirty socks; he'll slip away to make telephone calls
and she swears she isn't going to go through that
again, isn't going to break down crying or begging
nor is she going to scream at him, she's finished
with all that. And he's silent beside her,
not the kind to talk much but he's thinking
thank God he made the right move at last,
he's a little dazed like a man in a dream—
is this a dream?—so much that's wide, still,
mute, horizontal, and the counterman in white,
stooped as he is and unmoving, and the man

on the other stool unmoving except to sip
his coffee; but he's feeling pretty good,
it's primarily relief, this time he's sure
as hell going to make it work, he owes it to her
and to himself, Christ's sake. And she's thinking
the light in this place is too bright, probably
not very flattering, she hates it when her lipstick
wears off and her makeup gets caked, she'd like
to use a ladies' room but there isn't one here
and Jesus how long before a gas station opens?—
it's the middle of the night and she has a feeling
time is never going to budge. This time
though she isn't going to demean herself—
he starts in about his wife, his kids, how
he let them down, they trusted him and he let
them down, she'll slam out of the goddamned room
and if he calls her *Sugar* or *Baby* in that voice,
running his hands over her like he has the right,
she'll slap his face hard, *You know I hate that: Stop!*
And he'll stop. He'd better. The angrier
she gets the stiller she is, hasn't said a word
for the past ten minutes, not a strand
of her hair stirs, and it smells a little like ashes
or like the henna she uses to brighten it, but
the smell is faint or anyway, crazy for her
like he is, he doesn't notice, or mind—
burying his hot face in her neck, between her cool

breasts, or her legs—wherever she'll have him,
and whenever. She's still contemplating
the cigarette burning in her hand,
the counterman is still stooped gaping
at her, and he doesn't mind that, why not,
as long as she doesn't look back, in fact
he's thinking he's the luckiest man in the world
so why isn't he happier?

THE MOUNTAIN LION

The mountain lion with jewels for eyes entered, panting,
my sleep,
as if it were his own.

His saliva was sweet as honey,
flooding my mouth.

The mountain lion filled me like a hand slowly forced
into a glove—
tight, *tight.*
Now the jewel eyes are locked to my own.

• • •

I first saw the mountain lion in the Sierra Nevadas,
dun-colored, heavy switching tail, tawny eyes.
Idly trotting in the sun.
Asleep for centuries on sun-baked rock.
His breath hot and fetid,
smelling of blood.

The mountain lion's soul is transparent
as spring water.
If it exists.

• • •

In my dreaming head the mountain lion paced.
His wisdom was sudden as bones being crunched.

When he leapt his muscles rippled,
his splendid skeleton defined itself—
hunger in motion!—godly
in motion.

Passion ebbs as the stomach's sac is filled,
the mountain lion tells us.
He eats without tasting,
he sleeps with as little emotion
as he wakes.

His blood is warm as sap provoked
by sunshine.
My breath comes panting, hurting,
with such animal heat—

• • •

The mountain lion with jewels for eyes gnaws fiercely
at himself,
beset by lice.

His heavy-lidded eyes. His great wet sandpaper tongue.
Licking, stroking.
Gnawing.
Drawing blood.

An ancient legend—a god's weight enclosed
in rank animal heat.

• • •

The mountain lion stirs, and wakes,
and turns,
lazy and alert in the blinding sunshine.
If he has devoured human entrails
it was without passion
or sentiment:
only wet teeth gleaming,
eyes winking like jewels.

When I woke I was alone.
I am always alone, waking.
And at other times—alone.
Alone in the dreaming skull,
the precarious head.

The mountain lion trots idly in the sun,
in the soundless rain.

SPARROW HAWK ABOVE A NEW JERSEY CORNFIELD

This hawk in silhouette
    a razor's edge
        weightless
            sheerly black
                innocent as a scrap of paper,
                    forked to sail—
                        the black-feathered muscles
                            scarcely moving,
                                the eye
                                    unerring—
                        January winds
                            like waves washing
                        through the tallest trees—

                    We are crossing the snow-stubbled
                                            field

                in awe of
                    that singular motion,
                flawless, seemingly
        idle—
Life hunting life—

And the Sunday sky a hard ceramic blue:
                            Splendid bird!—
                                all theology reduced
                            to a beaked silhouette
                                gliding, idly
                    turning

        weightless
           as an eye's casual mote—
                But how splendid a bird!—
                      the eye
                  unerring—
              now rising,
            slowly banking,
         circling,
           and again soaring
             as if it were a benediction of the air
           and not life hunting life—

So the shadow of Death skims
  lightly
     the snow at our feet,
       the beak hidden,
         the silhouette taut
           with grace,
             innocence—
         Splendid bird whose blood isn't pricked
         by the sweet scent of ours—

NEW JERSEY WHITE-TAILED DEER

i
Your sin
is "overbreeding"—
the greed to populate the world
with your kind.

For this—
death by starvation.

ii
Prowling the January woods—
a skeletal forest, black-on-white,
Japanese in execution—
you exhale desire
in tiny spasms
of steam.

In startled sympathy
our souls fly after you:
a fiction that offers
comfort.

iii
Morning?—opaque
and dream-muddled.
And outside our windows
the snow is madly churned
as if by heraldic beasts—
not seven or eight starving deer,
all does.

iv
Tonight—last night—
the years before yesterday—
these childhood apparitions
accursed with useless beauty—
Pray for us.

Creatures of legend and perfection—
cloven-hoofed,
erect white "flags" for tails
for hunters' gunsights—
great-eyed
doe-eyed—
Pray for us.

v
That doomed fawn about whose neck
Alice slipped a graceful arm—
figures of earthen-furred beauty—
dun-colored,
camouflaged,
the finitude of heartbreak—
Pray for us.

vi
Your crashing flight
through underbrush—
and our souls *do* fly after.

vii
By January moonlight
deer disturb our sleep—
eating, chewing,
noisy,
ivy—vines—dried leaves—evergreen branches—
browsing,
starving,
outside our window.

Hunger, you teach, is promiscuous.
Hunger is dun-colored in beauty.
Hunger requires "camouflage"

50

but will become reckless, finally,
in the presence of food.

A secret most poetry disavows.

viii
(When I trotted to join them
my hooves, my sudden weight, broke through
the snow's hard crust.
Marvelous the strength
of these new muscles!—
the ease of great moist eyes
in their sockets—

The Eucharist crackles between our teeth.
It is tough, sinewy, dry,
mere briars.
It will not melt but must be chewed.)

NIGHT

We call *Night* the privation of relish
in the appetite for all things.
            —St. John of the Cross

She remembers the episode taking place at night.
It is a nighttime tale, an allegory perhaps;
she is seized from behind, a forearm across her neck,
snug beneath her chin. She is a child of eleven.

It happens so quickly, it always happens so quickly,
she hasn't time to scream. And then she hasn't breath.
It is night, she has begun to choke, she is losing
consciousness, she will forget.
Forgetting is generally recommended.

Her weight, in opposition to *his*, must be slight.
She will choke, she can't scream or sob; if she faints
perhaps his anger will be placated.
Nor does she tug roughly at the arm. Nor claw at the face.
(In fact there is no face, because it is night.)

He will not harm her. She is tall for her age, so
he might have been misled.
She often lies. She can't be trusted.
When she falls to the pavement (they are in an underpass
beneath the railroad tracks) he will release her.
She is not clinically "molested."

52

There is no blood except from her scraped knees.
There is no scar or enduring wound
except the nighttime tale, the memory.

It is always night, she cannot not remember it as night,
though wasn't it afternoon?—she was returning home
from school, descending the steps from the street,
an old route, absolutely safe by daylight.

Still, she remembers the episode taking place at night.
In which she will be proved, twenty years later, a liar.
As for the rest of the tale—isn't it fictitious?

You've always had too much imagination, she is told.

DREAM AFTER BERGEN-BELSEN

Did you know
the brain is glass
and glass can shatter,
and sift, and shift

and give such hurt
beyond imagining
so consonants draw out
to *Oooooooo's*

like mouths, or eyes
popped from sockets
of pain and push,
a band tourniqueted

round the head
to bring the blood
to boil, and past,
as in the Nazi doctors'

experiments for
"science" and—well,
for fun:
did you know?

"I DON'T WANT TO ALARM YOU"

I don't want to alarm you.
I know how hard a time you've had of it lately.
I know how, your back being broken, it's painful
for you to walk here with me
as if we were equals.

I know you try not to think about it.
And to forgive, where forgetting has failed.
It's the wisest strategy, I think, for you to assume
that air of subtly modulated hurt, a bit of dignity
in which no one much believes. Yet
saving face is courteous
and we thank you.

And if, these days, you are happiest
in that sea-green haze between sleep and wakefulness
where the body floats placid, paralyzed,
and blessed, I think too that is the wisest strategy
for you, for now.

MAKEUP ARTIST

"I feel like such a . . . shit.
I rescued this little lost terrier
on Broadway and Ninetieth, mangy little thing
that couldn't even bark, I took him home,
took him to the vet, nursed him back
to health or almost, then, Labor Day week-
end—my husband and I are separated, that's
the thing—I went to Atlantic City with a
friend and when I got back Skippy was dead.
I guess I'd sort of forgotten him, locked
in the kitchen, so much on my mind I forgot
to give him extra water and food and he never
did bark, just sort of accepted things. . . .
Look straight up at the ceiling now, I promise
I won't jab you in the eye."

PHOTOGRAPHY SESSION

—in memory of Jim Jacobs

You died on Wednesday. On Friday
I'm hauled by limousine to be photographed
for a magazine feature, Charles Street
near Varick, a garbagey smell to the air.
March 25 and warm as May! "My object,"
the photographer explains, "is an utterly
natural image." His five assistants, all male,
move like dancers in the semi-dark.

For years you'd kept your dying a secret.
The illness . . . its dread name. Chemotherapy
and blood transfusions and the rest. Sparing
us, one might say cheating us of premature sorrow.

Thirty minutes were required to make up my face.
Pain doesn't sweat at any pore, nor
does the meager soul reveal itself.
Layered in paste, paint, rouge . . . I'm safe.
"Look into the lens," the photographer says
patiently, repeatedly, "—look at *me*."

THE CONSOLATION OF ANIMALS

It's their not knowing how they must die.
The emptiness of their beautiful eyes.
The heat and damp and pulse of their breaths,
the way joy seizes them like a miniature death—
and no shame in it.

A WINTER SUITE

Winter Cemetery

Here, adrift in snow,
grave yielding to grave.
The chiseled words a braille of ice,
the old marriages erased.

An angel's pocked hand lifts in warning.
The head is encased in white,
the angry eyes are crusted over.
I am here! I am no other!

Why do we laugh suddenly,
fear exploding in tiny puffs of steam?
This is the catechism of winter—
here, adrift.

Winter Love

The roofs of all the neighborhoods are sagging with snow,
the chimneys of all the roofs are clogged,
snow sifts fine as sand in all the corners.

All the entombed marriages!—
snug and blind as burrows.

Winter Solstice

The year gone in hillocks of white,
white seas, sandbars, tides
frozen in motion—
that glassy interior.
The storm has died
into the purity of form.

This is the pitiless North we are afraid
we deserve—
the year gone in mouthfuls,
tiny bones,
skeletons.
This, our true finitude:
the soul crying a perfect O.

Winter Threnody

After twenty hours the snowfall stopped
without our noticing.

Follies of Winter

Here I am, I announced,
I've arrived at last—
driving day and night,
unsleeping—
I have been so good!

And they stared at me:
Who are you? And why?

Winter Wrath

Our rage is such that the very polar caps will melt,
when we have the power.
When we have the power.

Winter Boredom

The pocked face masked over.
Old landscapes, heaped in white, now new.
Winter is a fiction, so sheerly white,
its facets dazzle like truth.

But this is dirge music,
this is beggary,
do not be deceived.
Flat dead syllables like pebbles on the tongue:
the pocked face masked over.

Winter Aphorisms, Uncoded

Cut your throat!—counseled Jonathan Edwards' sermon.
Afterward attributed to Satan.

Husband, I whispered,
are those your eyes?

As for me—I turn the mirrors to the wall
and walk wherever I wish,
unobserved.

The mystery?—only a thin rubber sac
pulled from the skull and turned inside out.

Sly!—sly!—rumors and scandals
in the highest branches of the trees!

This thirst, husband, is only to be quenched
by opening a vein.

The love delirium was a tunnel we entered,
at Satan's bidding,
with only one way out.

Our house was one day exposed as four walls—a floor—
a ceiling.
We had believed it a great seaworthy vessel. . . .
("Madam, God himself could not sink this ship.")

We begged for God's special fire
until it rained upon us.

Black Winter Day

Why are you smiling,
as if you had the right?

Why, when it is December again,
that perpetual solstice?

Is it because the snow
is pocked, raddled, melt-
ing,
in black winter rain
through which
at unpremeditated intervals
crows fly pumping
their great clumsy wings—
and the rain continues,
hammering,
dripping,
in an ecstasy
of noise?

Winter Noontide

And the sun is ablaze,
again gay as a pinwheel.
Drunk with light.

And we too are drunk—
tottering on ice,
steamy breaths together,
gloved hands in gloved hands,
eager to forgive.

The sun *is* a child's pinwheel,
all innocence.
The sky is that hard enamel blue
that forgets so much.

The Thaw

With the tide of noon the long-awaited thaw begins.
No one is prepared.
An invisible drumming on all the roofs,
the underground caverns hollow with echoes.
Old reproaches, love murmurs,
drownings.
One moment is another moment suddenly aslant.

With the tide of noon the buried sea rises,
the long grasses begin to float.
The very air begins to pulse.
Even hurts, stitched over so long,
have become small glittering jewels.

    If you stand here where I stand,
not beside me but where I stand,
you would feel these slow-swelling tears.
This richness. This rejoicing.
That we melt,
we end,
we come again,

aslant,
not precisely remembered.
We will not be prepared,
we will be taken by surprise.

Small Hymns

The smallest of hymns, in praise of silk—
cornsilk, spiderweb silk—
those beings who slip, mere silhouettes,
through the cracks
of this exquisite moment—
and this—
and the next.

The Sacred Fount

This fresh cold rain is very much
the same rain as these slow-flowing
minutes are very much the same
minutes with vary-
ing words attached.
The hypothesis being
That makes all the difference!—
the varying words
attached.

Then again: this fresh cold rain
that shifts to mist and again to storm
and again to a wild hammering
on all the roofs of the world,
this sleet-rain, these filthy
chopping waves that float
the floorboards—*is* it very much
the same or altogether
fresh,
a new hypothesis,
solving nothing?

At last the chimneys are submerged.
All the horizons point north.
The bodies, freed, float.

YOUNG LOVE, AMERICA

III

YOUNG LOVE, AMERICA

Beside the Pepsi vending machine, red
white and blue, he's kneading her left buttock
through her bleached jeans hard enough
to bruise but she's kiss-tonguing
his ear, in play; you can tell
it's play since the orange façade
of HAROLDS TIRES 14^{95} is hot as the summer sun
at the horizon, and the sky, at dusk,
is just too blue.

He's wearing a shirt with sleeves rolled tight
to his biceps, an EXXON cap on oily curls,
her right arm crooked easy around his neck
like in the movies, smiling giggling teasing
hurting, in play, you know it's play
since the red-finned Plymouth at the margin
is distended as in a funky photograph
and the horizon's spiky, palms and eucalyptus
foreshortened at dusk. You know what? his white
teeth are saying, Us two could die together,
sometime.

NIGHT DRIVING

South into Jersey on I-95, rain and
windshield wipers and someone you love asleep
in the seat beside you, light on all sides
like teeth winking and that smell like baking
bread gone wrong, and you want
to die it's so beautiful—
you love the enormous trucks floating in spray
and the tall smokestacks rimmed with flame
and this hammering in your head,
this magnet drawing what's deepest
in you you can't name
except to know it's there.

WAITING ON ELVIS, 1956

This place up in Charlotte called Chuck's where I
used to waitress, and who came in one night
but Elvis and some of his friends before his concert
at the Arena. I was twenty-six, married but still
waiting tables, and we got to joking around like you
do, and here he was fingering the lace edge of my slip
where it showed below my hemline and I hadn't even
seen it and I slapped at him a little, saying, You
sure are the one aren't you, feeling my face burn, but
he was the kind of boy even meanness turned sweet in
his mouth.

Smiled at me and said, Yeah honey I guess I sure am.

ROLLER RINK, 1954

Looping & slamming & swinging their arms
Bobbie Sue & Vinnie & "I'm a Fool" rolling
wide on miniature wheels at the turn & back
& down & bearing hard on the cement track
& dust in our nostrils eyes ears hair lungs—
delicious! as Juicy Fruit & Fats Domino &
sweet little Lilia the minister's daughter
& Russ with the oiled hair in the red neon
stripes arms linked tight around each others'
waists in the careening dark & the roar of
the skates rolling wide like thunder as
the record shifts & for a heart's beat
there's silence   & you shrug it off,
dropping a dime for a lukewarm bottle of Coke,
& the first dreamy notes of "Ebb Tide" slide
on & who's this squeezing your scared sweaty
hand in his as the skate wheels roll round
& round & round, Christ don't let midnight
come & the music end & this roar as of
freight cars over & the fine powdery film
like death in the skull's cavities & coating
the pink tender lungs & the tongue too, spit-
ting & laughing in the parking lot & here's
the flat unmoving earth again: going nowhere.

AMERICAN MERCHANDISE

You wake to hear hurtling through the night sky freight cars,
missiles, helicopters, diesels bearing their precious
burdens!—each house on Cedar Avenue fully stocked but
there's always room for more. Rafters squeezed high,
     windows
opaque with goods, price tags carefully peeled away. This is
the land of birthdays. From the pulpit smiles of perfect white
teeth—*Do you pledge allegiance?*—fitted to every mouth.
Frank squat friendly Westinghouse refrigerator in the kitchen,
food in cubic inches, power throbbing in the VHS VCR
     and that
quivering code of antennae on the roof. Kelvinator
     GE   IBM
G & W   Buick Electra and Dow Chemical and Polaris
     under the
Christmas boughs—*The impossible in art,* says Oscar Wilde, *is
what has happened in "real" life.* A striped plastic tie for
Father he slips around his neck his expression unreadable but
his. And Mother lost in ecstasy amid the kitchen's secrets,
having memorized every dial, button, lever, slot. The word

processor is processing these words even as your lips shape them, and on tape in the TV the President and your Cedar Avenue neighbors welcome you to wherever this is. No other place for you if we've read you right! Even now the great diesels are headed in your direction.

THE HOUSE OF MYSTERY

Three nickels drop rattling into the till
and the North Clinton bus heaves
upward, a taste of brewer's yeast and
ashes, suddenly that tall narrow corner house—
the grainy dark of newspaper photographs—
two stories, an attic, and a basement
where the girl was kept—
and neighbors up and down the street heard nothing.
A day and a night, January 1953, another day
and a night, who knows how long,
music sometimes blared from the upper windows,
car doors were slammed at the curb,
a bottle smashed late at night
on the sidewalk, men's voices, laughter, who knows
how many, how many helped
in her death—
neighbors shut their windows tight
and heard nothing.

This is still a city of steep hills
where men and women wait in the freezing air
for buses—Main Street, Edgewater Park, East Avenue,
North Clinton and Clinton Ext.—streets of rowhouses
built to the sidewalk, no verandas
and no lawns, basement windows

opaque with the grime of years.
⟩ In my memory a fierce wet light strikes
the house's windows, an El Greco sky above
the house's steep roof,
but you can see it is an ordinary rowhouse,
wood-frame, shingled, needing paint,
there at the corner of Clinton and Fourth,
past which the buses heave.

The girl was fifteen, a runaway.
What did she expect, people whispered,
our parents told us nothing
and there was nothing we knew to guess
exactly—that blurred photograph in the paper,
confirmation, pageboy hair in the style
of that year, sweet-sullen mouth, pretty—
all blurred—so we stared
at the house of mystery
until the bus's windows steamed,
saying, There, that's it.
There. That's it. That's the house.

POEM IN DEATH VALLEY

Midday the light falls
straight as a knife.
The earth's too old
for love or pain
but what's to be done?

And what's to say
of salt flats shimmering
like water or ice
or a dream of God
we'd all suck on
if not for shame?

FLAME

—licking silently about
her brown shoulders beaded
with sweat as she runs
to no purpose in the
August street except
to get where she's going
and back again—
hot damp face and
black gems of eyes,
wild hair lifted
like flames so don't
touch me, *you*—

Don't even come near.

UNDEFEATED HEAVYWEIGHT, 20 YEARS OLD

I
Never been hurt! never
knocked down! or staggered or
stunned or made to know there's a blow
to kill not his own!—therefore the soul
glittering like jewels worn
on the outside of the body.

II
A boy with a death's-head mask dealing hurt
in an arc of six short inches. Unlike ours
his flesh recalls its godhead, if dimly. Unlike
us he knows he will live forever.

The walloping sounds of his body blows are iron
striking bone.
The joy he promises is of a fist breaking bone.
For whose soul is so bright, so burnished,
so naked in display?

All insult, says this death's-head—ancient, tribal,
last week's on the street—is redeemed in the taste
of another's blood.

You don't know. But you know.

1986

HOW DELICATELY . . .

How delicately the fish's
    backbone is being
lifted out of its
    cooked flesh—
the sinewy spine, near-

translucent bones
    gently detached from
the pink flesh—
    how delicately, with
what love, there can be no hurt.

HEAT

Late afternoon. Distant shouts.
Young raw voices, male, floating
in the heat. Are they angry, or
bored, or is it the heat shout-
ing through them? You forget where
you are sometimes, where
you've started from.

Dull grinding of machines, grinding to climax in red clayey earth
beyond the woods. This is the season
of small black inchworms that, when
touched, curl at once into balls
cunning as punctuation marks
on the stone walk, but
that won't save them.

MANIA: EARLY PHASE

How you love everything that flies
at you!—the world's in gear, food tastes,
colors bleed beyond their boundaries
but feel right, your tongue numbs
in anticipation. While others prepare
their statements: *We saw it coming.*
We were there, we saw. All the way from
the Caribbean, the Amazon, Cape Horn—
that lethal gale.

COMPOST

Heaped with the rinds and husks
of things devoured, the compost
is layered like memory yielding
to rot. Like loving

everyone who loves you, so
loving no one—it's safest so.
Old generosities of things that
didn't know they were dying.

Noon heat. Ferment. And the air
alive with flies, wasps. All's
companionable where shapes are
emptied out, hence shapeless,

nouns dissolving to verbs. Peel-
ings, blackened skins, muskmelon
rinds like sickle moons. And
the broken zinnias you'd have difficulty

remembering as gorgeous. On the dining
room table for most of a week, flamey
orange, scarlet to break the heart, but
we forget. Old generosities. Such heat.

LATE DECEMBER, NEW JERSEY

Between the railroad tracks
between the winter fields
four patches of orange, evenly
spaced, moving
with shotguns in the crooks
of their arms slow,
methodical, hunters' Day-Glo
hats, dickeys so
comical in intention,
bringing only,
after all,
death.

FISH

When you stand on the bank awash
in sun the fish dart slant-
wise through your upraised hand,
all gold, glinting, nerve ends
quicker than flesh so
be humble. Don't even try
to change your life.

IN JANA'S GARDEN

—for Jana Harris

Here, in July, in Jana's weedy garden,
heat rising from the earth like vapor
and such luxuries of vegetables!—
red onions and parsley and peppers and
beets and mint and lettuce newly bolted
thigh-high and sweet corn in tall shaggy
rows and potatoes unearthed like crude
gems heaped in our arms—and thank you,
thank you for every gift this life we
haven't deserved and now at harvest,
when the air pulses with heat and the sky
is massed with fat dimpled clouds like pride
licking itself unrepentant, hungry
for all you can give.

THE
TIME
TRAVELER

THE TIME TRAVELER

By degrees, days
and years,
another voice
intrudes.
Another presence.
The facial skin betrayed
by old smiles.
Death's-head nostrils,
too deep.

Behind the eyes—
another inhabitant.
Candles entrusted
to trembling hands.

I don't recognize
that person,
you whisper,
who is that person?
A stranger's face
swimming
in a mirror.

In remembered dusk
strolling behind
the boarded-up
train depot—
broken glass,
scattered papers,
weeds—
tall sinewy weeds—
but the flowers
tiny, pinched,
exquisitely blue—

To have the luxury,
now, of picking a
mere handful!—
a mere handful.

SLEEPLESS IN HEIDELBERG

In Der Europäische Hof on the
          Friedrich-Ebert-Anlage
where, in 1937, on a wildly successful
          tour of southern Germany,
Adolf Hitler stayed, night is translated
          into German. Serrated sounds
of plumbing, mysteries

in the walls, floorboards
          overhead. Voices and
laughter and if only you could
          sleep! if only there were
sleep, what couldn't you forgive,
          or countenance, or do!
Nazi doctors too

suffered breakdowns sometimes.
          They had their bouts of anxiety,
nervous tremors, diminution of appetite, self-
          doubt. Sleepless too
like you, thinking how human beings will do
          anything to one another, the proof
of it being *we have done it.*

Anything thumb and forefinger can devise!
   In the name of green romance
of the Odenwald, romance of ancient
      druidic stones. And those gorgeous tiers
of gardens above the Neckar where beauty
      renews itself each season. Not forgetful
because new and not doomed to be forgotten

because, merely, doomed—and forgotten.
   Hitler too was sleepless probably
after such deafening applause, thousands of faces
      streaming ecstatic tears. Fresh forms
of old oblivion and who can blame him?—the globe
      proffered as on the tremulous nose
of a circus seal. *Take and eat.*

STRAIT OF MAGELLAN

For two nights fevered you haven't
      slept whispering *Strait*
of Magellan. Golfo San Jorge.
      Mar del Plata. And why not
set sail?—that dreamy feathery

lilt to the horizon means
      your frail ship won't sink
nor will your bones be picked
      clean by the shriek-
ing sea birds in your wake

that eat when they eat and
      sleep when they
sleep. Such efficient
      beaks! Along the coast
the surf is thunder and

rage, clean, your sails sucked
      hollow. No world but
waves heaving saw-toothed
      and aqua, exquisite
as Japanese woodcut waves but

can you sink in them?—can
      you sleep?—
the sun crazed in facets
      as a great fly's
eye fixing you

in its stare?
      Boredom, it's said, is
not wanting to know
      how much you hate what
you don't know you

hate because
      you love it,
but how can that be you?—buck-
      ing the serrated waves
of the Strait of Magellan.

MINIATURES: EAST EUROPE

The surface of the earth
is paved with tombstones—
flat, worn smooth,
glistening
with rain.

   •   •   •

Here it is our faith
that the code can be cracked.
Though the secret is all surface.
"Think of a defective heart
hanging outside the rib cage
of a newborn infant. . . ."

•   •   •

The American sojourner
in East Europe:
where we are "not ourselves."
Cultural ambassadors,
emissaries of art,
sincerity. . . .
Our heads ring with too many bells
extolling too much history.
Gamely persisting in handshakes,
smiling through translators,
staring at tiny withered apples

heaped in sidewalk bins—
a feast! a feast!—
for the imagination.

•   •   •

In Warsaw,
in the great green damp parks,
flocks of *kös*—
black-feathered birds
resembling robins—
pick in the grass,
unobserved.
Their song,
unknown in North America,
is so exquisite
you think at first
you must be mistaken.

Then you hear them everywhere:
kös—black robins—
unknown in North America.

•   •   •

Chopin's piano was smashed in the street
by Russian soldiers:
but his heart
(now an official relic)

is entombed
in a Warsaw church.

In rural Zelazowa Wola,
where Chopin was born,
recorded preludes and mazurkas
are piped to an assemblage
on the grass.
There is the awkward pretense—
which we Americans observe—
that the music is being "played"
inside the birthplace shrine.

•   •   •

Death seepage
from the Jewish cemetery—
its vast incalculable acres—
now a tourist attraction.
As for the Warsaw ghetto,
long paved over, now an apartment complex,
"It was not distinguished architecturally;
it is no great loss to Warsaw."

Another time
an official remarks,
"Poland is now 97 percent pure—
so far as race
is concerned."

• • •

In East Europe,
Pascal's divinity redefined:
"The center nowhere,
the circumference—the barbed wire—everywhere."
• • •

Starving
in queues,
anger turned to stone,
the population dreams
not of freedom
but of food:
freedom *is* food,
food *is* freedom.

"It is difficult to say the spiritual consequences
of prolonged hunger. . . ."
• • •

Idle, self-stymied,
sickened in stasis,
the American murmurs
I want to die.
It is a genuine prayer,
in its idiom.

The citizen of a slave state prays
I want to die as a slave.

•   •   •

"Is suicide rare
in occupied zones?"

"Yes—the state takes care of it."

•   •   •

How intense it is,
how wakeful,
life in occupied zones!
As if one were being
constantly filmed:
each handshake a riddle,
each locking of eyes
an entire "theory of being"—
though the secret is all surface,
the malformed heart
outside the body.

•   •   •

In Budapest
where a coppery-toned Hilton
emerges from a medieval monastery—
all rock, plate glass in vertical strips,
heart-stopping Danube views—
slave chambermaids
in sturdy peasant bodies
appear and disappear
by way of secret stairs,

passages:
cherry-red lips,
plucked and penciled eyebrows,
knee-high woolen socks,
laced-up canvas boots
(with inexplicable
open toes and heels):
a cheerful army,
all muscles and stealth.
Pale straining legs,
strong shoulders, arms,
knotty veins raised
on the backs of their hands,
emerging from passageways,
murmuring their secret language.

"But they're automatons,
they look right through us. . . ."

• • •

In occupied zones
the entire world is a text,
and all are readers, in thrall.
Where freedom dissipates meaning
or the terror of discovering it,
freedom's absence intensifies meaning,
meanings—

but how to unknot them?
Cyrillic, codified:
even the hapless clouds participate,
spiced with native poisons.

We try,
we try very hard,
to swallow without gagging
the lukewarm "cream-based"
clotted soup,
as our interpreters watch.

● ● ●

The lobby of the Europejski Hotel,
coils of cigarette smoke,
nervous Polish laughter,
conference delegates arriving and departing,
always arriving and departing,
always the hour of tolling bells.
It is rumored that a "nonperson"
has been operated on for cancer
of the throat,
but none of us
can pronounce his name.

Grease and fried onions.
Grease and fried onions.

It is always the hour
of tolling bells,
always the hour
of grease and fried onions,
rumors, laughter, shrines to Our Lady.

●   ●   ●

"The Jews could have saved themselves—
some of them—
if they had made the effort.
But they were too lazy."

●   ●   ●

Gradually, by hours and days,
we are "not ourselves."
We are mimes, smilers,
objects of curiosity,
objects of much fawning solicitude
and much hatred.

"The Americans as a people adore travel,
the Americans are always passing through. . . ."

●   ●   ●

"You are the most *American* of writers,
man or woman—
so it is said?"

●   ●   ●

This language,
haunting to the ear,
sheer music,
devoid of meaning:
the compound sentence
with its many variations,
its subordinate and coordinate clauses:
water rushing
along a rocky stream,
tumbling and falling,
dropping,
dissolving to spray. . . .
Words made music,
eddying about our heads. . . .

It is always our faith,
American,
that the code can be cracked.

"I must be telling lies,
I smile so often. . . ."

•   •   •

The ear listens
but cannot think.
The eye sees—
the eye is engorged
with seeing—
but cannot think.

How, then, to remain human. . . ?

• • •

The American,
exulting in freedom,
sinks into the body,
into the "singularity" of the body—
its moods, its surprises,
its drifting ideas,
its mirror religion.

The slave citizens,
trapped in slave states,
slave histories,
dream of walls to be scaled,
of food,
flight,
the triumph of the "real."

"But if I leave Poland
I will leave my language. . . .
I am not sure that I know myself
without my language."
So a young poet mused
as the walls were being erected.

AN OLD PRAYER

A person to be writing a tale, and to
find that it shapes itself against his
intentions; that the characters act
otherwise than he thought; that un-
foreseen events occur; and a catas-
trophe comes which he strives in vain
to avert. It might shadow forth his
own fate,—he having made himself
one of the personages.

—Hawthorne,
American Notebooks, 1835

The stories that require telling. The stories that insist
upon their telling. Bud and flower in the brain and crack
the brain like concrete. The syllables, the words,
the intoxication of ink, the old mossy tales,
engraved in stone.

Crossing the room just now you experiment inviting
a story: the high-polished floor, the rap of the heels,
a stir of seductive curtains at the window, the moon
curved small as a fingernail.
If you lean out the window to seize the moon:
a story, an ancient story, teeth sinking
in your throat.
Don't imagine you are master.
You are never master.

And how must it end? you ask.

MUD ELEGY

—in memory of Bill Goyen

Late summer. And the pond is mud.
Rivulets of mud, fleshy mud, a curviform alphabet of mud.
The dragonflies glitter like needles,
the wasps' angry drone has its logic,
and the frogs (leaping frantic, eyes bulging like gems)
if they could blame us would blame us. . . .
All's mud; nor are we out of it.

The long months of your dying
I wandered the pond's weedy edge,
no words,
nothing to say,
no spell to cast.
The pond shrank slowly to mud,
the heat haze smelled of rot. . . .
Pockets of shallow water teemed with life
even as it disappeared.

The mud elegy is loss and grief
but mainly helplessness,
the stupor of bloated frog bellies,
the film easing over an eye. . . .

The mud elegy has its dignity
though it is mainly mud.

Small deaths do not matter
except to what is small.

This heat haze is stale as air already breathed,
but we won't stop breathing it for that reason.
The mud elegy is obliged to make that point.

We don't have our pride.

HONEYMOON: FORTY YEARS

Tarpaper roof, and the floorboards like something floating.
The silo was a black funnel stained with swill.
I laughed, and the sound ran out into the fields
like summer lightning. Do it to me again, I said,
and you did.

The bubble in my thighs became a head, and hard,
and hurt. Damn big man, even your thumbs hurt.
Giggling on the cornhusks there to be hurt.

       Mostly the years are just dry sounds rattling
in the fields, old jukebox songs up the highway. Thistles
where the kids' pony grazed. Tiny blue eye burning
in the gas stove. Some of them telephone and some don't.
Send cards or don't. I could count but I don't.
Nothing on TV or the picture's bad or we need some voice
not here. I'm waiting for you to die so
I can remember you kindly.

THE FLOATING BIRCHES

He'd been coughing so hard a rib cracked,
and now the brace grips him like
a shrewd hand. *Hey. I got you.*
I know all about you.

One night, needing to urinate,
he gropes for a shoe.
But the shoe isn't under the bed.
He lifts himself weightless
and goes to the farthest corner
of the room where there's a fence
and beyond the fence a field
of junked cars—
he hadn't known were there!
But the hot stream splashes
and falls short, wetting his toes,
and he begins to cry knowing
there's a mistake
but not how to make it right!

This good woman my wife 50 yrs. is innocent
of any & all wrongdoing of Mine. She knew
nothing of transactions of any financial kind
nor of moral misdeeds & crimes. All
I forgot, I confess & sign my name.
She must not know of this or any

of the children as ALL ARE INNOCENT
& I only am to blame.

They lied, saying it was an ambulance,
but up the driveway comes a hearse.
The bedclothes tangle,
the pillow flies to the floor.
Such rage! such hurt! then
there's sudden dignity in surrender
and a disdain for the daughter
who grips his naked foot,
clipping toenails thick as horn.
And the other who prepares the corpse—
washing the wasted sides, the belly
and shrunken testicles, and
the hollow of the thigh where by night
the angel wounded with a touch.

One by one, our faces framed
in his hands, one by one,
in the reek of the bedpan,
a father's blessing.

And now the slow drive through the countryside
by moonlight, the white birches floating.
He's happy, the heart's muscle relaxes.
No one can regret this world in which,
on hillsides, the white birches
float. . . .

"I CAN STAND THERE IN THE CORNER . . ."

—for Norman Sherry

March 13, on the Gulf of Mexico above
Corpus Christi, Texas . . . staring out
at the turbulent water, blue, white-
crested waves; the ceaseless crash
of surf; a hazy cloudless day
like Eternity—depthless and dull.

Yesterday, rain; today a harsh white-
glaring sunshine; tomorrow, fire
ravenous to burn the earth . . .
or indifferent, like both fire
and earth.

Why are we here? is a question
not to be asked. The world beyond man—
wiry grasses, sedge, clayey dirt, bleached sand—
the gulls that circle and rise and fall as
they've done eternally, screaming
at one another in a semblance
of rage—is perfect, complete: thus
Why are we here? We, aching with imperfection
like nails grown ragged.

We want a vocabulary larger than sky,
earth, shifting shadows, the Gulf, God.

We hunger for irresolution, for hurt.
This beauty of which, in homage, I should
write, in fact does not move me much.
Instead I am thinking of a story told me
the other evening at dinner: the aged,
wizened, badly stammering Somerset Maugham
on the Riviera, maybe drunk or in some way
deranged—out of loneliness? bitterness?
self-loathing? or, indeed, perfectly normal,
like you and me?—telling a visitor,
"I am a small man. I can stand there
in the corner, and maybe Death will not see me."

IN MEMORIAM

—in memory of Blanche Woodside, 1894–1970

And why, don't ask. Why,
you can't know. I was crying and
she said, But I don't mind. The eyelids translucent, a bone of an arm
you didn't want to see, but
she didn't die that afternoon,
or that week.

Leading, as they say, my own life.
Those long months. One day
watching with bitterness a friend
approach on the street—in Windsor, Ontario—
until by degrees he turned into
a man I didn't know.
The quick fear, then, that
everything would go, for
who was to prevent it?

Those months. Years. *A circle
with its center everywhere, circumference
nowhere:* all I want to remember
of Pascal's God.

•   •   •

In the city of her death I am always
fourteen years old, dreaming in Woolworth's
window. Those startling reflections
that float toward you out of glass—
you hope for perfection
to bear you forward.
Don't smile. That vision. As in later years
a November storm will do it—
leafless trees in the morning, suddenly a new
brilliance to the sun everywhere
flooding the house.

Fourteen years old: she didn't know was it
her body she wanted to starve into submission,
or her soul. Which angered her more.

And why, and how, their curious linkage.

The day she died I stood in the parking lot
amid the windshields and chrome, the dirty
asphalt, mute, weak, stupid, you look but
you don't see, someone calls your name but
you don't hear, the usual. Above, a sky
so hard and blue it looked all surface, something to be calmly touched.

•   •   •

114

Those years. There's a photograph
of the South Korean boxer Duk Koo-Kim
taken on the last night of his life.
Las Vegas, November 13, 1982. Bowing low
before his opponent Ray Mancini in
formal apology for having fouled him.
That image floats toward me: the doomed man
covered in sweat, exhausted, composed.
The fight will go fourteen rounds
before he's released. To be counted out
is to be counted out of Time and the instant
comes when you know you inhabit madness,
you are the very vehicle of madness, but
it's the instant you await and if
it doesn't come you're exhausted awaiting it,
and no release. He was a warrior—hadn't
he written in Korean *Kill or be killed*
on a lampshade before the fight?—and a final
blow of Mancini's broke a blood vessel
in his brain. And when he came back to earth
he placed himself at the margin of light,
the edge of what's called consciousness.
Evil, says Kafka, does not exist. Once
you have crossed the threshold,
all is good.

And why, don't ask. You can't know
except to ask. How to cross over
in dignity? in terror? in resignation?
in pride? in cowardice? in irony? not
as you'd hoped to be but as you are?—
that last consolation.

I don't mind, she said. And I keep hearing.

The face is still floating in Woolworth's window
where so many faces float. The glass
has long since been shattered, the block of old
buildings razed, new smart rubble of glass and
concrete and jazzy orange brick erected in its place.

FALLING ASLEEP AT THE WHEEL, ROUTE 98 NORTH

—in memory of John Gardner

Now it happens the other cars begin to float.
You've been driving too many hours with old griefs
rising like sleep rising, guilt heavy
on the eyelids. Seconds away from death *by accident*
by automobile but such peace, you can't believe
it would hurt, north above Manchester, N.H.,
but you don't know the mileage or
how long. Trees at the roadside blurred
as their names. *Why can't you remember*
saying goodbye? you're thinking.
Smooth rushing pavement at 70 mph.

        Of course there was a final time
you'd kissed, in parting. Always is. Old friends saying
goodbye, not guessing it really is
goodbye. His arms slung around your shoulders,
wet and bearish his breath, yes, and drunk,
and this time it was final but you can't remember.
(Early those evenings he'd be drunk, floating.
Long pale tangled hair floating.
Pale eyes fanatic and kind and
he'd forgive: he knew of surviving,

and guilt, and hating
what's nearest,
mirrored.)

      He'd been driving his motorcycle when he died.
Not drunk and not drifting off to sleep
like this. And not suicide,
just *lost control* they said *at the curve*
they said, as a way of saying
how, why. For what else can be said?—
this old story always new,
piercing the bowels.

So you tell yourself, drifting
off to sleep at the wheel,
as the other cars float
reflected in the windshield
and darkness spreading like warm soft mud
though you'd walked with such care
in the little brook . . .
in the clear transparent water.

  •   •   •

If it was a swift startled death it was a good death
for that terrible hour and for that stretch
of Pennsylvania highway hundreds of miles to the south,
but you're wanting it not to have happened quite yet and
maybe it hasn't happened quite yet, or
not exactly in that way. And
falling asleep at the wheel in speed,
in wind, in the caress of winking lights,
you guess it might only have been
something you're dreaming. A way
of getting from there to here,
tonight.

LAST EXIT BEFORE BRIDGE

Memory. That place we invent where
what never happened in quite that way
keeps happening. Keeps
happening.

There was once a young woman lying
at the side of a highway. So public and
was she a woman like you you didn't want
to know. A "traffic accident,"

and her car crushed "like an accordion,"
skidded sideways against the highway
divider. Uniformed men, an ambulance,
one of those ceremonial occasions

where four lanes of traffic are funneled
into three, red flares, sirens, a migration
of vehicles inching westward at the blinding hour of 6 P.M. when the sun blazes

off chrome and windshields and everyone
was staring at the young woman whom
they couldn't see lying in shattered glass
weeping, or bleeding, or is she dead?—

about to be lifted onto a stretcher but
it's too insignificant to be noted
in the newspaper and no one will remember
it as it happened—just east

of the great Tappan Zee Bridge where
shattered glass is promiscuous and if
there's an accident it's another crushed car
and if there's blood on the pavement

it's someone else's blood, or merely
oil stains. So it's pointless to return
one day years later pointing, *There.*
There. Spiky weeds the color of grit,

concrete, no urgency even from the sun,
no memory except where, when the windshield smashed, your head and that certainty
came so perfectly together.

LOCKING THROUGH

May 9, 1987, was declared "Joyce
Carol Oates Day" in Lockport, New
York, the poet's birthplace

Where the Erie Canal's steep rock walls
contemplate each other—amid the racket of white
water that's angry or happy,
depending upon the sun—
and the great locks are locked tight
as jaws that will not, God damn you,
will not give—
the tugboat floats tethered in water
leaden-green as old moss,
choppy, deep, between
the steep rock walls like silence
above the boat of banners, flags whipping
in the wind,
and such merriment!—
the official boat carrying the mayor
and his wife and his aides and honored citizens
and media people crowded in the prow,
in the cabin, along the narrow sides;
a trio too of violin, accordion, lusty horn
playing "Stars and Stripes Forever,"
"Let Me Call You Sweetheart";—where
Father Joseph McCarren blesses the boat
that is all boats on the Erie Barge Canal,
the stretch of waterway that is all waterways,
the citizens of Lockport, New York,

who are all citizens
of our great nation—
"On land and on sea, by day and by night,
Bless us O Lord and these thy gifts"—
taking from his pocket a pint-sized bottle
of holy water to sprinkle deftly
at our feet: "Amen."

And we shiver in the sun as the music dies
and the boat begins to sink with the green water
draining out of the thirty-foot lock,
and there's quiet, a chill,
as of something suddenly recalled
but not named,
as we drift downward
and the steep rock walls rise
damp and implacable above us
to resume their old contemplation of each other.
"In the bright ignorant air. . . ."
We have dropped below the sun, the fierce May wind
cannot touch us as the great locks slide open
and the waterway beyond is revealed
unpeopled as a Dutch landscape, or
Death's kingdom. We stare as if knowing
what it is we see.

"In all, we will drop sixty feet. There is no
going back." And in the distance
the next set of locks, locked tight as jaws.
And the little boat shudders and moves forward.
Our brief journey begins.

WEEDY LOGIC

—for Tess and Ray

Shaken and jubilant at the edge of the woods knowing
we'd seen Death but Death had not seen us.
And that night midnight jazz from San Francisco, saxo-
phone, trumpet, notes so pure the future
became suddenly possible.

Friends living their lives year following year,
disasters at their feet, small ignoble failures like
wood shavings they kick aside, seeming not to notice
and why not? The logic of survival.
Why not.

Oh, Jesus, he was speaking of the beauty of white.
The mad white rim of the eyeball above the iris.
Ice. Ivory. Paper. Snow. White-walled rooms
with white-framed windows fixing the Absolute.
How present tense resolves itself whitely to past.

Don't look. *Don't* look—circling the dead deer
at the edge of the woods: a doe, and how mute. And
how heavy lying on its side, the girth of its belly
that seemed swollen, stiffened legs, the gaping muzzle
and a bright buzz of flies. And wonder seized us.

That morning of grasses now Death. The fresh-painted
room smelling of Death. Steam rising from gratings
in the street that is Death but mysterious, the way
the poem is always a love poem, always in love with
its subject—helpless, chagrined. The way fireflies

drifting against the window demonstrate that the Absolute
doesn't matter. Do you know, he said, that sensation
driving into a city you've never seen before, mile upon
mile of houses, streets, *So many human beings who don't
know us* and it's a child's amazement denied at once,

like the discovery of jewelweed, named because of the glittering drops of moisture at the corners of the leaves
in the early morning, or daisy, named for the day's eye,
the creek you'd see as a child miles from home and someone would say, There, that's our creek! and you'd have

to take it on faith, so much existence wider than you
know. And plaques for the dead, like poems no one reads,
crusted in birdlime and the birds close by with their
sun-sparked song, persisting, *It's always the same morning!*
And why not? Already the asphalt is cracking, giant
weeds pushing up from beneath. Weedy logic.

THE ABANDONED

Did the hands have a name that built the grape arbor
behind the abandoned house in Salamanca, New York where,
at dusk, in October, we trespassed—rotting trellis overhead,
leaves curled like treble notes, vines like wires
and the pea-sized shriveled grapes no one has wanted,
not even the crows?

THE MIRACULOUS BIRTH

Christmas: the house adrift in a wide white ocean of snow.
Black December is a ditch winking overhead,
but here beneath your parents' roof the piecrust faces
are dimpled by forks
and the clock faces are round and smooth as buttons.

This is the season of waiting and of expectation
and of hunger keenly roused to be satisfied.
This is the season of the miraculous birth,
the oldest story,
these years,
centuries—
the fresh-trimmed spruce bristling to the ceiling,
smelling of cold, of night, of forests wild and tamed
as forests in a child's picture book.

The splendid tree is balanced in a shallow tin of water
looking as if it would live forever—
green-spicy, sharp-needled—
and such tinsel, such trinkets ablaze
on the boughs, a glass-glitter
of icicles, angel's hair,
strings of colored lights plugged to a socket!
And beneath the tree presents wrapped in shiny paper,
satiny bows, gifts heaped upon gifts—
a child's fever dream spilled on the carpet.

Outside, snow flying like white horses' manes and tails;
inside, cookies that are stars, hearts, diamonds,
the smell of a turkey roasting slow in its fat.

There are stories children are not told,
of grandmothers dying in secret of their hearts
or of cancer shopping for months for this season—
the costly boxed gifts that are love, the stiff silver paper
that is love, all the effort of joy, love—
torn open too quickly by a child's impatient fingers.
And there suddenly is your father,
young again,
entering the kitchen, the wind behind him,
snow melting in his wild dark hair,
a carton of presents in his arms.

From what and to what could this world be redeemed?
is not a child's question.
You are sitting at the long table with the others.
Those years. The roof weighted with snow. Candle flames,
the smell of red wax, oh, take and eat; the clock tells
its small rounded time again
and again, again—
this is all there is and this is everything.
The miraculous birth is your own.

ACKNOWLEDGMENTS

The poems in this volume have originally appeared, often in different versions, in the following publications. My thanks to the editors involved.

Agni Review: "Don't Bare Your Soul!", "I Can Stand There in the Corner," "American Merchandise"

American Poetry Review: "Honeymoon: Forty Years"

Antaeus: "Compost"

Atlantic Monthly: "Young Love, America"

Bennington Review: "Luxury of Being Despised"

Boulevard: "Locking Through"

California Quarterly: "White Piano"

Denver Quarterly: "Miniatures: East Europe"

Georgia Review: "Poem in Death Valley"

Grand Street: "Your Blood in a Little Puddle, On the Ground"

Hudson Review: "The Time Traveler"

Iowa Review: "Love Letter . . . ," "Winslow Homer's *The Gulf Stream*, 1902"

Kenyon Review: "Mud Elegy"

Malahat Review: "Black Winter Day"

Massachusetts Review: "Night Driving"

Michigan Quarterly Review: "New Jersey White-Tailed Deer," "Roller Rink, 1954," "Sleepless in Heidelberg"

Missouri Review: "The House of Mystery"

The Nation: "Strait of Magellan"

New Directions: "A Winter Suite"

New England Review: "How Delicately . . ."

The New Republic: "Fish," "An Ordinary Morning in Las Vegas"

The New York Times Magazine: "The Miraculous Birth," "Sparrow Hawk Above a New Jersey Cornfield"

Ohio Review: "Last Exit Before Bridge"

Ontario Review: "Dream After Bergen-Belsen," "I Don't Want to Alarm You," "Flame," "The Abandoned"

Paris Review: "Makeup Artist," "Photography Session"

Ploughshares: "The Consolation of Animals"

Prairie Schooner: "Undefeated Heavyweight . . ."

Santa Monica Review: "The Floating Birches"

Sewanee Review: "An Old Prayer"

Shenandoah: "Mania: Early Phase," "Peaches, Pineapples, Hazelnuts," "I Saw a Woman Walking . . ."

Southern Review: "The Mountain Lion," "Self-Portrait as a Still Life"

Southwest Review: "Loves of the Parrots"

TriQuarterly (a publication of Northwestern University): "Playlet for Voices," *"Marsyas Flayed by Apollo,"* "Whispering Glades"

2 Plus 2: "In Memoriam"

Western Humanities Review: "Welcome to Dallas!"

Yale Review: "Heat," "Edward Hopper's *Nighthawks*, 1942"

"The Sacred Fount" appeared in a special limited edition, *Luxury of Sin*, Lord John Press, 1984.

"Small Hymns" appeared as a broadside, William B. Ewart, Concord, New Hampshire, 1983.

"Falling Asleep at the Wheel, Route 98 North," appeared in a special limited edition, *The Time Traveler*, Lord John Press, 1987.

"In Jana's Garden" appeared in *Portraits of Poets*, 1986.

The unnamed presence with "manly fingers" in "Love Letter, with Static Interference from Einstein's Brain" is the Princeton psychologist Julian Jaynes.

The "undefeated heavyweight" in "Undefeated Heavyweight, 20 Years Old" is Mike Tyson before winning the first of his titles.